DATE DUE

MAY 05		

Brodart Co.	Cat. # 55 137 001	Printed in USA

Keeping Secrets

by Tormod Haugen

translated from the Norwegian by
David R. Jacobs

illustrations by Donna Diamond

HarperCollins*Publishers*

First published in 1976 in Norway under the title *Zeppelin* by Gyldendal
Norsk Forlag, Oslo.
First published in 1991 in England and Australia under the title *Zeppelin* by
Turton & Chambers Ltd, Station Road, Woodchester Stroud, Glos GL5
5EQ, England, and 10 Armagh Street, Victoria Park, W. Australia 6100.

Library of Congress Cataloging-in-Publication Data
Haugen, Tormod.
[Zeppelin. English]
Keeping secrets / by Tormod Haugen ; illustrations by Donna Diamond ;
translated from the Norwegian by David R. Jacobs.
  p.   cm.
Translation of: Zeppelin.
Summary: Her encounters with the mysterious boy who lurks near her
family's summer cottage and her discovery of the "magical" word, zeppelin,
cause ten-year-old Nina to see her parents in a different light.
ISBN 0-06-020881-3. – ISBN 0-06-020882-1 (lib. bdg.)
[1. Parent and child–Fiction.   2. Behavior–Fiction.   3. Runaways–
Fiction.]   I. Diamond, Donna, ill.   II. Title.
PZ7.H2866Ke   1994   92-8319
[Fic]–dc20   CIP
                                                                AC

Typography by Daniel C. O'Leary
1   2   3   4   5   6   7   8   9   10
❖
First American Edition, 1994

1

Eva and Martin and Nina.
Mother and father and child.
A family.
A happy family.
They had just about everything, said Martin:
a home and a car and TV and a vacation house and
—and they had each other.

2

A smiling mouth is a happy mouth.
A frowning mouth is a crabby mouth.
Smile in the eye, a smile so mild.
You're the lucky one, my child.
You have smiles where your knees bend
and even where your toes end.
If you don't smile now, you may be left behind.

3

Happy people should smile, said Martin.
Eva and Martin often smiled with their lips.
When Nina was around, they smiled all the time.
But their eyes seldom smiled.
Nina had noticed that.

4

Even if you forget that one and one make two,
you must not forget the kindest thing to do.

A bedtime song when Nina was little.

She was good whenever she did what her parents wanted.

She was bad whenever she did what Nina wanted.

Happy people are good, said Eva.

So Eva and Martin were kind to each other, and to animals and friends.

They were good parents, they said.

Nina tried to be good, because then she was happiest.

5

Nina had a bad dream, even though she was good.

She didn't dare tell anyone about it. Sometimes she would wake from the dream and cry. She asked God to take the dream away. But it came over and over again.

Someone was chasing her.

She was running, but she didn't seem to be moving.

A tall thin man in a black cape.

He was getting closer and closer.

Long arms and white fingers reached for her.

Suddenly she was holding a stick.

She hit him again and again.

The man fell and he was bleeding.

It was Martin.

Nina screamed and woke up.

She didn't understand.

How could she hit her father, who was good?

6

If there are angels, they look like Nina, said Uncle Ole.

Nina thought about glossy postcards covered with glitter.

Glossy angels covered with glitter were the worst thing she knew.

7

There was a Nina who stole money and bought chocolate.

There was a Nina who hit Jonas several times, so hard that he bled.

There was a Nina who deliberately broke Aunt Ria's fine ashtray.

Nina didn't really know this Nina.

The Nina whom Martin and Eva loved didn't do such things.

Nina didn't like the stranger who came and pretended to be her.

Nina wanted to be loved.

8

Nina had Ria's chin and Otto's cheeks.

Grandma's ears and Grandpa's toes.
Martin's eyes and Eva's hair.
Gitta's legs and Ole's back.
Nothing was Nina's.

9

Once the lights went out.

Pitch blackness.

Martin and Nina in the living room. Eva in the kitchen.

Completely quiet.

"Martin?"

He didn't answer.

"Martin!"

Eva's voice was not Eva's. It was as if someone else were speaking.

A gust of cold air passed through the living room.

Then the lights came on again.

Nothing to be afraid of, said Martin.

I wasn't afraid, said Eva.

But Nina heard that she was afraid.

10

That terrible time.

She was six years old and ran away from home. She didn't remember why anymore. The rest she would never forget:

Night came, and darkness.

She cried and was alone.

A policeman found her and took her home.

The lights in the window were good.

The door was safe.

But Eva was crying, and Martin was standing white and stern behind her chair.

"Nina," they said, "Nina, how could you do this to us? How could you frighten us so?"

She was punished. She had to go to bed without a comforting word or supper or a warm hand against her cheek.

Something happened to Nina that day.

She still didn't know what it was.

Maybe someday she would work it out.

11

Things Nina didn't understand:

Once in a while angry voices coming from behind a closed door.

Once in a while the sound of crying from the bedroom when Eva was alone.

Once in a while Eva going to bed even though Martin had still not come home.

Once in a while the long silences between Martin and Eva.

All this happened once in a while.

Eva and Martin never mentioned it to Nina. Perhaps it was only something she imagined.

After all, they were happy.

12

"When I was a child," Martin often began.

Then Eva would look at him with despair.

"You sound as if you're a hundred years old," she'd say.

Martin never knew how to go on.

He often left the room.

13

"These are my parents," said Eva, and dusted the black frame. "Nina, can you see I am like my mother?"

Nina looked and shook her head.

Eva looked for a long time at the picture.

She looked deeply into the picture.

"I wish I weren't," Eva said in a low voice.

Nina didn't understand what she meant.

14

Monday the tenth of July, eight o'clock in the evening.

Something happened then that neither Martin nor Eva nor Nina understood.

A good day for Nina.

It had been busy with Sylvia and Jorunn and play.

Not once had they quarreled.

"See you tomorrow," Sylvia had said.

"Yes," Nina had answered, and been full of pleasant thoughts.

But she had forgotten. Tomorrow was the summer vacation house.

She went inside and remembered it.

Then she heard herself say: "I don't want to go."

What she heard was terrible.

Martin and Eva looked at her. They didn't say anything.

A long, black silence.

"You must pack your things," Eva said at last.

"Yes, Mother," Nina answered obediently.

The sound of the terrible words disappeared.

They behaved as if she hadn't said what she had said.

As if everything were the way it should be.

Monday the tenth of July, at eight o'clock in the evening, Nina had said dangerous words.

She was ten years and two months old.

She woke up in the night and knew that she had said the words.

She knew it was wrong.

At the same time, she knew it was right.

A long time passed before she fell asleep again.

15

". . . and mow the lawn and weed the flowerbeds," said Eva.

"—and water properly and paint the shed," said Martin.

"—and cut the hedge and clear up the dead

leaves," said Eva.

"—and paint the garden chairs and mend the gutters," said Martin.

"—and go to fetch more gravel . . ."

The chores of paradise, said Martin.

The joys of vacation, said Eva.

In the backseat Nina slept while they drove farther into the summer.

16

Summersummersummersummer—

Summervacationsummerhousesummerexpectations—

Vacation = no problems.

Vacation = away from the daily routine.

Vacation = happiness.

In the front of the car sat Eva and Martin. They filled the summer with everything they would do.

Their summer.

They had never asked Nina what kind of summer she wanted.

Nina's summer would have to be their summer.

17

"We're here! Nina, wake up!"

The car stopped.

The vacation house was still there.

It was just as it had been last year.

Or the year before.

Nothing had changed.

This year like last year like the year before:
The same chairs to be painted.
The same flowerbeds to be weeded.
The same grass to be cut.
The same—
"Help me unpack, Nina," said Eva.
Martin had already gone inside.
Nina got out of the car.
She stood on the same gravel path as last year. The same small stones.
Eva smiled at her.
Her summer smile.
The same one as last year.
The smile that went up into her eyes.
Suddenly a shout came from the house.
A frightened shout.

18

"Martin!"
Eva dropped the suitcases and ran toward the house.
Nina ran after her.
They stopped in the doorway.
"Martin, where are you?"
"Here," came the answer from the bedroom.
They ran up the stairs.
Eva stopped at the door. "Martin, what—"
She interrupted herself with a gasp.
"Was it like this when you came in?" she whispered.

"Yes," Martin answered in a low voice.

Nina pushed past Eva into the room and saw:

19

Someone had been lying in the double bed.

The comforter lay in a messy heap in the middle.

On the bedside table were several chocolate bars. One of them was half eaten.

Martin bent down and picked up a pair of blue sneakers.

"What in the world . . . ?" began Eva.

Martin shook his head. "I don't know."

They looked at one another. They stared over the bed at Nina. They searched each other's eyes.

Nina felt their alarm.

A little gust of cold air crept into the room.

They didn't notice that she was looking at them.

She was outside them now.

A chill ran down her back.

This was something that happened to other people.

Something you read about in newspapers.

But it couldn't happen to them.

20

"This is impossible," said Eva, "but it looks as if someone has been living in our house."

Martin nodded.

"But who?"

Martin shook his head.

"I have never seen anything like this," said Eva. "I can't believe my eyes."

"I'll call the police," said Martin. "This can't be happening. This is our house, this is our bed and no one can live here without our permission."

"What if—they are still here?" said Eva.

None of them said anything for a while.

Creeping footsteps and whispering voices filled the quiet, thought Nina. She went farther into the room to stand between Eva and Martin.

"I shall look through the house," said Martin. "Stay here until I come back."

Nina's room was empty. Martin thundered down the stairs as if he were trying to scare someone away. They heard him run through all the downstairs rooms.

The cellar door was opened, and the footsteps disappeared down the steps. Soon after, Martin was with them again.

"Nothing," he said.

"Nothing," Eva repeated.

21

The shoes seemed to glow with a blue light standing there on the floor.

They were pointing at Nina.

They had looked big when Martin had picked them up. As though they belonged to giant feet. Now they

seemed almost ordinary. Almost friendly.

Dangerous?

Nina wasn't sure.

So odd that the shoes had pointed at her.

So odd that they had shrunk.

Dangerous?

If she took four steps, she would be able to touch them.

She took four steps and did touch them.

It was odd to hold the shoes. They were so distinct against her fingers. They looked like ordinary blue sneakers. But they were different. Something about them had frightened Eva and Martin.

There was writing in red ink over the instep on the right shoe.

It was blurred, but after a while it became a word.

Zeppelin, it said.

Zeppelin.

"Nina, drop those awful shoes! Go and wash your hands at once!"

Eva's voice crackled hysterically at her.

Nina was startled and dropped the shoes as if they could bite.

A hard thump on the floor.

Frightened, Nina looked at Eva.

Eva stared back without a word.

22

The summer house was a house full of light.

During the day in the sun.

At night because of the moon.

In the sunlit days the rooms were golden.

Against moonless nights, the house was closed up tight with curtains.

The total darkness menaced the house of light—

23

A single safe dark place in the house.

Nina had found it and claimed it for herself.

In the innermost darkness under the stairs between upstairs and downstairs.

An alone place. A thinking place. A dreaming place.

Nina was afraid of the big darkness.

But the little darkness under the stairs was safe.

24

Zeppelin—

The word glowed in the dark under the stairs.

The word smelled like flowers at twilight and tasted like vanilla ice cream.

Zeppelin—

Like something out of a fairy tale.

Hocus pocus, abracadabra and open sesame for treasures hidden in holes and caves.

Fairy-tale treasures.

But *Zeppelin* was there on a real blue sneaker.

Nina didn't dare say the word aloud. Perhaps it would lead her into the magic mountain.

Best to be careful.

Zeppelin—just a little thought.

The word glowed.

Nina closed her eyes and let it sink inside her.

How odd—

It was as if the word fell into place beside her.

25

"Nina, where are you?"

Out of the darkness. Into the light.

"Here I am."

"You mustn't frighten me so. I thought something had happened to you. I want you to stay with me until Martin comes back from the police station."

They sat at the kitchen table.

In the middle of the day.

The sun was shining.

Insects and birds.

A light wind.

Outside it was safe and good.

Inside there was a cold draft along the walls.

"Can't we go outside?" asked Nina. She sat and listened for sounds in the house.

"No, it's safest to stay here until Martin comes

back," Eva replied.

26

Nothing had been stolen.

Nothing was damaged.

Nothing could be done, because no one knew anything or had seen anyone.

Wait and see.

"Wait and see?"

Eva looked at Martin.

"A lot can happen while we wait and see."

She was cross and losing heart.

"No, we can't protect ourselves against strangers who want to threaten us," Martin said angrily. "We'll have to work this out for ourselves."

"The shed," said Eva.

"You're right," said Martin, "we forgot to look there."

They went out into the day and the light and the wind and the birds.

It was pleasant and warm outside.

27

Eva and Martin went into the shed.

They didn't see Nina go outside.

She walked into the garden and stood by the fence at the back of the house. Eva and Martin couldn't see her.

Nina stared at the path that curved enticingly

under the dark spruce trees.

The path went on and on.

She stood still.

All at once she felt it.

Someone was looking at her.

The *stare* glided over her back and tickled her neck. Her scalp itched.

Slowly she turned round.

No one. Nothing.

But someone was looking at her. She tried to meet the *stare*, but where should she look?

She let her eyes sweep over the garden.

She tried to see through the bushes.

She tried to peer through the foliage.

Come out! she thought, but no one came.

She stood and waited. With her back to the fence. To the path. To the woods. To the darkness under the trees.

It was as if the day grew dark and the light turned pale and the wind grew stronger and the birds shrieked.

Suddenly she knew that something big and black was creeping along the path.

Eva's fear.

Martin's worry.

Perhaps it was safer inside after all.

The path grew dark behind her.

The eyes held her prisoner.

It must be *zeppelineyes*. She had believed they were

friendly, but this was a black, hard *stare*. Eva and Martin had been right.

If only they would find her before the black creeping thing came and licked her back.

"Nina!"

Martin's voice.

Nina relaxed. Her feet could move again.

She smiled.

The black creeping thing shriveled up on the path behind her and turned into a puddle that grew pale in the sun. Soon it was completely gone.

"Nina, there you are! Didn't Mother tell you to stay with us?"

It didn't matter that he was angry.

Nina went toward him, and she still felt the eyes.

But that no longer mattered, because Martin had come to rescue her.

28

Go or stay?

A house where danger lurked and mystery dwelled.

A house where terrors watched and riddles went unsolved.

Best for Nina—

Safe and sound and good and warm and snug.

"But this is our house," said Martin. "We own it. Shall we allow ourselves to be terrorized by intruders? We have to stand up for ourselves! We must not give in. What kind of world would this be if we let ourselves be frightened by wickedness? I will protect you with my life if necessary." Here he cleared his throat and began to speak more softly. "I vote for staying here."

Eva and Nina sat on the sofa.

Eva nodded without a word.

Nina nodded too.

29

It was not because Martin was brave.

Not only because he wanted to protect them.

Not only because he spoke so recklessly.

It was those things too.

But mostly it was the word.

Zeppelin—

Nina couldn't tell them that.

30

Martin changed all the locks in the house.

He made sure that all the windows were properly shut.

He made sure that all the doors were locked.

He made sure and then he checked again.

He promised to stay alert that night.

The light would be left on in the hall.

The doors would be left open between the two bedrooms.

It was safest to sleep with closed windows.

Now let the night come—

Suddenly Nina started from sleep.

A sharp whistling sound came from the garden.

Martin was beside her in a flash.

"What is it?" asked Eva.

"What is it?" asked Nina.

"I don't know," said Martin. "Maybe an animal."

"No," said Eva, "it's the owner of the shoes. Perhaps he's going to break in to get his shoes and chocolate and—"

Her voice rose. It grew different and high-pitched until it cracked and she was quiet.

Nina heard that Eva's voice made the shadows darken and spread, pressing around the house.

"It's him," said Eva.

Nina hadn't thought about whether it was a he or a she or a they.

"Martin, we have to do something!" cried Eva when she got her voice back.

"I can't see anything," said Martin.

Invisible, thought Nina. There was something out there in the garden, and it could creep in between the cracks in the walls and suddenly be inside.

Martin turned away from the window. "Nina, you should come and sleep with us for the rest of the night."

He went back to Eva. Nina stood up and went to the window.

32

The garden was gray and swaying.

The flowers stood colorless. The treetops grew black against the white heavens. The bushes were gray wool, the spiraea heavy with summer snow.

Then she caught sight of the shadow gliding away from the maple tree.

She wasn't afraid. She wasn't nervous. It was as if she knew what she was going to see.

The shadow was still for a moment.

Something white. A face lifted itself toward the window. She recognized the *stare* she had felt during the day.

A hand waved. To her. At her.

Then the shadow moved and became part of the bushes.

"Nina, are you coming?"

"Yes . . ."

She felt light and strange. As if she too were swaying. Like the garden and the shadow in the night.

The *zeppelinshadow* had shown itself.

It wanted something from her.

She was afraid. She was not afraid.

She lay between Eva and Martin. Long after they had fallen asleep, she stared into the dusk, a little gleam of light within her.

33

Next morning there were no footprints in the garden.

Nothing to find.

As if no one had been there.

As if the shadow had floated.

Strange, said Eva and Martin.

34

All three of them had looked at the big shoes.

But Nina had seen that they were small.

All three had heard the eerie whistling.

But Nina had seen the shadow that whistled.

All three had experienced the same thing.

Nevertheless, it was different.

Nina saw a little more than Eva and Martin.

35

Midmorning stillness.

Martin was painting the garden chairs in the middle of the lawn.

Eva was pulling weeds in the flowerbeds beside the walls of the house.

Nina went about doing nothing. But that was normal. No one to play with. Nothing to do. The usual.

A sound from the maple tree made her look up.

She started.

At first she wanted to call to Martin and Eva. But she had lost her voice.

She tried to pretend it was nothing.

She pretended she didn't see a naked foot on the branch.

She pretended she didn't see the sun-bronzed leg disappearing among the green leaves.

She pretended that nothing flickered on a red shirt between the branches.

She stood there and pretended that it was a completely normal tree without a foot or a leg or a red shirt.

But the foot and the leg and the shirt were there.

She stared at the foot.

She knew it.

She was looking at a *zeppelinfoot*.

But what should she do—?

She looked at Eva bent over the flowerbeds.

She looked at Martin bent over the garden chairs.

They had been like that for quite a while.

As if everything were peaceful and good and safe.

Without suspecting that everything had changed in a second.

A voice came from the tree:

36

"At last! I thought you would never come!"

Horrified, she looked up.

Horrified, she looked down.

"I know you've seen me, but I saw you first."

Nina didn't say anything.

It wasn't Nina who was standing there. It wasn't Nina he was talking to.

"I was sitting in the tree when you arrived yesterday."

Nina said nothing.

Martin painted and Eva weeded. How could they!

A sigh from the tree: "Can you speak?"

Someone nodded.

It must have been Nina who nodded.

"I was afraid you didn't have a voice. Can you say yes?"

"Yes," answered the odd and distant voice. It was Nina's she heard.

"Can you say anything else?"

"What are you doing in our tree?" asked the distant voice that must be Nina's.

"Yours? Is your name written on it?"

"It's growing in our garden, so it's our tree!" The distant voice was angry. "What are you doing there?"

"Sitting."

"Why?"

"Because this is a fine tree to sit in. I've tried out every tree, and this is the best."

Martin painted and Eva weeded.

Either they were a dream or Nina was.

"Are the— Do you have—blue sneakers?" asked the

distant voice.

"Yup."

"Are they the ones we found in the bedroom?"

"Yup."

"Why are they there?"

"Because I'm sitting here without them."

"But what are they doing in our house?"

"Nothing."

"Yes, but they are there," said the normal Nina-voice. She gave a shudder. She hadn't realized that she had come so close again.

Dream or real—

Martin painted and Eva weeded.

"Yes, yes, they're there," answered the voice that sounded real.

Nina felt the wind on her arms and legs. The sun burned her skin, and freckles were coming out on her upper arms. She heard the insects and the birds. All that must be real.

Her voice was still far away. But his voice was close by. Perhaps he was real. And Eva and Martin and the garden chairs and the flowers as well. Perhaps she was a dream walking in the garden—

Actually she should be afraid and call Eva and Martin. But she wasn't exactly afraid. And she didn't call.

The voice close by spoke again.

"That's why I've been waiting for you."

"Why?" answered Nina far away from herself.

"So that you'll fetch my shoes. My feet were freezing during the night."

"Do you sleep in the tree?"

It was only in dreams that anyone slept in trees.

"It's a fine tree to sleep in, if you want to know. There's a hammock and a table and everything I need up here. Except my shoes."

"Why don't you sleep in your own house?"

"Perhaps I don't have a bed. Perhaps I don't have a home. Have you thought of that?"

"No—"

"But I can't tell you."

"Why not?"

It was so easy to answer. Nina heard herself answer. But she didn't know what she was going to say until she heard her voice.

"I can't talk about such things without shoes on."

"I don't dare fetch them."

"They won't bite."

"No—"

"They're so nice, really. Just pat them first, then they'll come along with no problem."

"I don't have permission to fetch them."

"You have permission from me."

"I don't have it from my mother and father."

He looked carefully at her between the leaves. She

recognized the *stare* from last night.

"Who do the shoes belong to?" he asked.

"You."

"Correct. Then your parents have no right to steal my shoes."

"I don't dare."

He looked at her.

"I don't dare to."

"Won't you even try?"

Eva straightened up and looked at Nina.

"What are you doing?" she called.

"Nothing," Nina called back.

So it was really real. She was just as real as everything around her.

"You look as if you're talking to the tree. Why don't you find something interesting to do?"

"Yes, Mother."

"Can't you try?" whispered the voice in the tree. "It isn't dangerous. I'm sure of it. If you won't do it, I don't know whether I'll speak to you anymore. Just remember that."

A little glimmer. A little light.

A little vibration passed through her.

Nina turned around and walked across the lawn.

"Where are you going?" Martin called after her. His voice reached her like an echo.

"Just inside for a minute," someone answered.

"Why?" That must have been Eva.

"I'm getting a book," someone answered.

With every step she was leaving reality.

37

The vacation house was a dream house.

She opened the dream door and went into the dream.

She floated up the stairs. Her feet moved almost without touching the ground.

Slow arms and slow feet.

The bedroom door swung open by itself. As if it were ready for her.

The shoes were waiting in a blue light that filled the whole room. She had blue arms and blue legs.

The shoes were pointing at her.

She sank down onto her knees in front of them. They glistened and shone like the *zeppelinword* within her.

The red letters were clear now. Like small flames rising from the shoes. Warm against her hands. A scent of twilight flowers.

Then her hands turned white. They looked like snow hands.

Slowly they stretched themselves out toward the shoes, as if they were moving in water.

She touched the shoes.

At first they were hard and cold against her fingers. Then the blue color thickened and the shoes became soft and dreamlike.

Slowly, slowly she picked up the shoes and put them under her blouse.

Out of that room. Into her room.

Down the stairs with a pile of books.

Then she glided into the piercing sunlight and out of the dream.

38

"Have you brought all your books with you?" asked Eva, too close.

"Yes." Her voice was unclear. "I didn't know which I wanted to read."

Grass under her feet. Branches overhead. She stood under the tree.

She put the books down. Eva and Martin weeded and painted.

Out with the shoes. Up between the branches. The boy took them.

His hands brushed against hers.

This was no dream.

Nina's forehead and hands were sweating.

She felt a pain in her stomach.

She had to sit down.

"What is it?" whispered the voice from the tree.

She didn't answer. She looked at Eva and Martin. They kept on with their work as if nothing were happening.

They didn't suspect that a boy was sitting in the tree.

They didn't suspect that she was doing something they didn't know about.

Nina didn't know if she had permission; she'd done it without asking.

The pain was worse.

Like stealing. Like lying. And they didn't know anything about it.

She got up and ran across the lawn.

"Nina!" called Martin.

"Nina!" called Eva.

She didn't stop. The tears came, and she was sick behind the biggest currant bush.

39

"Nina, what is it?"

Two shadows fell on her.

Hands stroked her hair. Gentle hands. The sweat dried on her forehead.

"Are you ill?"

She couldn't answer. Her throat was choked with sobs.

"What's the matter with her, Eva?" asked Martin.

"I don't know—Nina—"

She cried and cried.

They stood helplessly watching.

"I don't know," Eva repeated. "She always used to

tell us what was wrong."

The hands were there again. The gentle hands that caressed and comforted.

Her body shook under the light fingers.

The comforting hurt.

40

Afterward it was impossible.

"Why are you crying, Nina?"

"There must be a reason!"

"You can't cry like this for no reason."

"Did you hurt yourself? Did you get stung?"

"Nina, we just want to help you."

Nothing worked. She couldn't tell.

"Nina, you know we trust you. We get worried when we think something is wrong."

"Are you afraid because someone has been in our house?"

She shook her head.

"Nina—you must not hide anything from us. We are only thinking of your own good—"

Then they didn't say any more.

All three sat silent. Nina looked down at the floor. Eva and Martin anxiously watched her and looked fearfully at each other.

"I don't understand anything," sighed Eva.

Martin, bewildered, shook his head.

Late evening came.

The blue light outside and the twilight inside.
Bedtime.

The doors were locked and the windows closed.

"The shoes are gone!" shouted Eva.

"It can't be true!" said Martin.

Both refused to believe what they saw.

"It's impossible," Martin said at last. "Shoes can't walk away by themselves."

"No one has come in here," said Eva. "We have been near the door the whole day. There must be a ghost here."

"Ghosts don't exist," Martin said seriously.

"Then how do you explain the disappearance of the shoes?" Eva said angrily.

"Poor Nina," Martin said softly. "We'd better not tell her. She'll only be frightened."

"You're right," Eva said just as softly.

Nina lay there and heard them talking together in low voices. She heard what they were saying.

Martin came in to her. "It's best that you sleep with us again tonight," he said, and lifted her up in her comforter.

Nina bored deeper into the comforter. Her body trembled.

"Poor child," said Eva. "She's crying again."

Crying?

A kind of bubbling in her throat that could have

been laughter.

Suddenly she was wide awake.

"Now this has gone far enough!" Martin shouted.

He threw himself out of bed and lurched down the stairs in his pajamas.

"I will not put up with this!" he yelled.

Eva and Nina ran into Nina's room and looked out the window. But they couldn't see who had whistled.

Martin went dashing out. He was like an explosion in the stillness.

He ran all over the garden.

Between the trees and around the trees, between the bushes and around them. Looked up and down, bent branches aside and looked.

"Where are you?" he called. "Come out. I know you're here!"

"What's going on?" a man on the other side of the street yelled.

"Is there something wrong?" a woman next door called out.

Martin stopped short, as if he had just realized what he was doing. He hurried inside again before anyone saw him.

"Is someone there?" the woman called again, but no one answered.

43

"There is nothing to laugh about," said Martin when he came upstairs.

"We're not laughing," Eva said seriously.

"It was for you I did that," said Martin.

"You were wonderful," said Eva. "You were brave to run outside in the middle of the night."

They went into the bedroom again.

"Nina!"

She was looking out into the garden. Searching for a shadow in the floating grayness.

"Nina!"

She was searching for a sign. For a wave.

But the garden was quiet.

"Nina, what are you waiting for? Come on now!"

"Okay."

A last look into the night.

Nothing between the wool bushes and the snow spiraea.

44

Next morning.

Good to wake up. Good to stretch out.

At first the world was only Nina in bed.

Then the whole room came into view. The window. The sunlight.

Thoughts floated outside into the summer. Over the flowerbeds. Over the grass. High in the maple tree.

Nina sat up with a jerk.

Yesterday—

Hadn't it happened a long time ago—?

She wished it were a thousand million years ago.

Because then it wouldn't have been Nina who had taken the shoes.

45

To take without permission was to steal.

Nina knew that.

But the shoes were not theirs.

She lied when she didn't tell anyone.

She knew that.

But just the same, she didn't think that she had lied.

It was so difficult.

46

"It really is a strange story," said the policeman at their kitchen table, "but there's nothing we can do."

"We're nervous about it," said Eva.

"It's worst for Nina," said Martin.

All three looked at her. Nina felt her face turn red.

"If only there were someone who knew something definite—" said the policeman, and looked at each of them in turn.

"You can go outside for the moment, Nina," said Martin. "This is not your problem. But don't go far, so we can see you from the window."

47

She didn't want to go over to the tree.

She went over to the tree.

She didn't want to sit down.

She sat down in the grass.

She didn't want to look up.

She looked up into the leaves.

Not a sound from the overhanging branches.

Not a bird.

She didn't want to sit there.

But she kept on sitting.

"I didn't believe you would come back," said the voice from the tree.

Nina jumped. But she wasn't really afraid.

She looked up.

The blue shoe and the leg and the red flickering.

She didn't answer.

"Your father can move fast," he said.

She didn't answer.

He came down a branch farther.

"Why did you run away yesterday?" he asked.

She didn't answer.

"Have you told your parents about me?"

She shook her head.

"Why didn't you?"

She shook her head.

That was something she didn't know.

48

Then his voice grew happier:

"I hope I'll enjoy myself here."

"What do you mean?"

"I thought I might settle down here for a while."

"Where?"

"At your house. You can give me food and a home. Just now I want lots of food. Slices of bread with lettuce and jam and ham and cheese—but not goat cheese, because I get that in my school lunches, and now I'm on vacation."

"If you promise to tell me what you're doing here."

"I can't do that."

"Then there'll be no food."

"You can't just let me starve to death."

"I can."

Nina felt sure of herself. She spoke with his voice. Now she was the one who made decisions.

"Are you going to explain or not?" she asked.

"I don't think so."

"Then there'll be no food."

"That's just great," said the boy. "I might as well disappear, and then you can believe that you dreamed me."

The leg disappeared into the tree.

49

"No, wait!"

Nina heard herself shout.

Confused, she held her breath.

Perhaps she was not the stronger, after all.

The leg returned. The blue shoe shone above her.

"Do I get food now?"

Nina nodded and stood up.

50

If only she could understand—

She became so afraid when the leg and the shoe disappeared.

When *zeppelin* pulled his foot back into the leaves.

As if the boy would never come back.

As if she were going to lose a—friend.

51

Nina went across the lawn, over the gravel path, up the steps, into the kitchen.

Yesterday had been like a dream.

Today it was real.

It was Nina who opened the refrigerator door. It was Nina who took out the hamburgers and potatoes from yesterday's dinner. It was Nina who got out crisp bread and the package of processed cheese. It was Nina who put everything into a plastic bag.

And she did it without being afraid.

Steps in the hall.

"Nina?"

It was Martin.

Suddenly it became dangerous.

He mustn't see her.

Out through the living room. The veranda door stood ajar.

She pushed it open. Fortunately it didn't squeak.

"Nina!"

She was stealing, she was stealing, she—

She remembered Martin's stern white face from long ago.

That time he had come in and found her with money in her hand.

Money she had taken.

Their Nina didn't do such things.

Nevertheless she was doing it.

Did she not belong to them?

But surely they had each other—

Tears almost coming. Sweat on her hands.

Quickly over the lawn. Under the tree. Up with the hand. Slowly as in a dream again. An arm came down. The plastic bag swished up between the leaves.

"Nina!"

She turned around.

Martin stood on the veranda looking at her.

"What are you up to?"

There was no answer to that.

He was big. She was little.

He got bigger. She got smaller.

Martin tried to look into her mind. She couldn't

return his gaze. She became red and warm while he stared.

"What is it, Nina?"

She shook her head.

Martin waited. Far, far away. Like a giant she could never escape from.

52

"Nina, please, you're such a good girl."

Nina was not so good.

"You're worrying us so much."

She was not bad, either.

Eva and Martin were serious.

They hadn't smiled for two days.

What had become of their happiness?

53

All at once it was like two summers.

The safe, normal summer of Eva and Martin.

That summer was full of things they should paint and trim and weed and repair.

The other summer had blue *zeppelinshoes*.

Eva and Martin could not weed away the shoes. They couldn't repair away the whistling. They couldn't paint over the *zeppelinshadow*.

One summer for Eva and Martin.

One summer that wanted something from Nina.

54

"Martin, come here!"

He found her in front of the refrigerator.

"What is it, Eva?"

She didn't answer, and he looked inside the fridge.

"Where are the hamburgers and potatoes?" he asked.

"I don't know," said Eva. "I haven't touched them."

"Nor I," said Martin.

They looked at one another.

"He comes and goes as he wishes," said Eva.

"How does he manage to come inside without being seen?" said Martin.

Neither of them could answer that.

55

Suddenly everyone knew about it.

The news was out, and people stopped and talked and talked.

A little place where news travels fast.

One person had heard, and the second knew.

The third had heard from the first, and the fourth had heard from the second.

The news flew. It grew, became big, bigger, biggest. It fluttered from mouth to ear, from mouth to ear, from—

Then it cycled to the first person again.

Big exciting news that the first person didn't recognize anymore.

So it wandered further, from mouth to ear.

No one had heard anything like it.

No one could understand.

But then suddenly many had heard something just like it.

Then there were many who understood.

The neighbors were the first who came to Eva and Martin.

Over and over again Eva and Martin told them what had happened.

The reports varied from time to time.

The neighbors nodded and nodded.

One of them had heard terrible shrieks coming from the garden last night. Several had heard them.

There was one who had seen someone lurking outside his windows.

Several had seen someone lurking, now that he mentioned it.

They began to talk about burglary and theft and terrorism.

Then Johannes from Moen came and said that his bicycle had been stolen.

Then Gerda from Lund said that someone had been in her pantry and had swiped a whole ham and lots of bread.

Then Svensen said that someone had been in his hall and had taken a long black raincoat he was fond of.

They talked and talked and talked.

Fear lay behind it all.

After a couple of hours the whole neighborhood knew about the frightening things that had taken place.

The frightening things they couldn't explain.

56

The police were in despair.

Suddenly too many people knew something.

Eva and Martin were relieved. Suddenly everyone had information.

Nina was confused. She understood nothing. Something was wrong.

Everyone was talking about the shoes and the mysterious intruder. But she didn't remember the shoes as being so evil. Neither did she remember that the whistling had been so terrifying.

It was as if they were speaking about something that had nothing to do with her.

The adults also spoke about break-ins and thieves. They talked as if they knew. As if theirs were the only true story.

But it was wrong. It had to be wrong! Could the boy in the tree really be a thief?

They talked more and more. The adults knew so much. Perhaps they knew everything.

And Eva and Martin—Nina didn't understand what they were talking about. She didn't recognize their story.

Then there was the bicycle and the food and the raincoat.

A tall thin man in a black cape.

Nina had believed that he existed only in her dreams.

But now it seemed he had jumped into reality.

She didn't want to believe it, but the adults talked and talked. And she realized what they were thinking. They were thinking about a tall thin man in a black raincoat who bicycled around the streets in the middle of the night and whistled.

Why did he whistle?

Nina knew.

He whistled to children. He whistled to her.

The tall thin man was the boy in the tree.

He had transformed himself.

The magic word.

Zeppelin—

She had believed that it was a good word.

But it was certainly bad—

It was Nina he was after.

Did he want to catch her? To eat her?

It wasn't so—it couldn't be so! It had better not be so—but the adults said—all the adults said—but she knew—adults were right—

Nina crept into the safe darkness under the stairs.

The adults' words buzzed angrily from the

veranda.

It wasn't like that—it wasn't—

Exhausted, she sat there and didn't know what she should believe.

57

Zeppelin—

Good or bad.

Kind or evil.

Nina didn't know.

She closed her eyes and thought about the maple tree.

A tall thin man in a black cape was sitting there and waiting.

She tried to think of the boy in the tree. But he wasn't sitting there any longer.

The tall thin man had come out of her dreams. He was alive. He wanted to catch her.

There was only one thing to do.

She crept out of the darkness.

58

Martin walked around the garden.

"Father," said Nina, "I know where the tall thin man is."

"Tall thin man—?"

"The one you're looking for."

"Nina, what are you saying?"

He grabbed her by the arms. "Why haven't you told us this before?"

"He—he scared me so that I didn't dare."

"Did he—do anything to you?"

His voice was afraid.

Nina shook her head.

"Where is he then, child?"

"In the maple tree."

"In the maple tree?"

For a moment he looked suspicious.

Then he ran over to the tree.

"Is anyone there?" he called.

No one answered. There was no one to see.

Martin swung himself up onto the lowest branch.

"What are you doing?"

Eva came out with Liv and Sven, who lived next door.

"Nina says there is a man sitting in the tree."

He disappeared up into the leaves.

Everyone stared anxiously after him.

Martin shook his head when he came down again.

The others laughed a little.

"Children's fantasy," said Sven. "You must see that no one would be so stupid as to hide in a tree in your garden!"

He laughed, shaking his head.

He patted Nina on the shoulder. "Oh Nina, Nina, you make your father do such stupid things."

Martin was embarrassed.

"You must not fantasize so," he said. His voice was a little angry.

"It's so easy to tease you," said Eva, and laughed.

"There is obviously more than one person who has fantasies," said Liv.

Martin turned red in the face. He glared at each of them in turn. Then he grabbed Nina hard by the arm and shook her.

"This is not something to joke about," he said, and dropped her just as quickly as he had grabbed her.

The adults walked toward the house again.

"Don't go anywhere by yourself," called Eva before she closed the door behind her.

Nina was alone again.

Her breath stuck in her throat for a long time.

Then it loosened in big gasps.

No one believed her.

She was alone in the world with a tall thin man in a black cape.

59

Her heart beat.

Thump thump.

She heard it in her head.

It beat out a word.

A rustling, glowing word.

Zeppe-lin-zeppe-lin-zeppe-lin-

Meek and careful.

Kind and good.

Or was it hard and evil?
Nina didn't know.
But imagine if it were gentle and good.
Imagine if it were the boy in the tree.
A friend of sorts.
Then what had she done to him?

60

Suddenly—
A glimpse of red behind the peonies.
A lean black form crouched low.
She couldn't run into the house.
She couldn't run into the street either.
He was coming to get her again.
The path was nearest.
She turned and ran past the spiraea and the currant bushes.
She snatched open the gate and went up the path.

61

As she had run in the bad dream.
Heavy legs. Slow steps.
The rustle of the black cape behind her.
In among the black spruces.
Toward the middle of the forest where the night lived. The big dangerous darkness.
A shout flew past her.
Zeppelin—and the path vanished.
She turned into the tall ferns and green day.

Suddenly the stream was there and she was standing in the middle of it.

Up again on the other side.

A black rustling between the ferns behind her.

She looked back.

Red lightning zigzagged between the fronds.

Then he stood on the bank.

The boy from the tree. The tall thin man with the black cape.

He on one side of the stream.

She on the other.

62

"Why are you running like that?" he asked, out of breath.

Nina didn't answer.

"What are you afraid of?"

She didn't answer.

"Answer!"

He took a step toward the stream.

That was the signal.

She started to run again.

63

She didn't get far.

Long arms and white fingers knocked her down.

Nina screamed and held her hands up against the *zeppelinstare*.

"What is the matter with you?"

It was not the voice of the tall thin man.

They were anxious words from the boy in the tree.

"What have I done to you?"

Frightened blue eyes peered between her fingers. Gentle eyes.

She burst into tears.

He didn't say anything, only looked down at her in confusion.

64

When the crying grew quiet:

"Are you the boy in the tree?"

"Yes, I'm the boy in the tree."

"And you're no one else?"

"No, I'm no one else."

"And can you transform yourself?"

"No, I can't transform myself."

"Prove it," she said.

"Well, how?" he asked.

She pushed herself away from him. As if she were trying to creep out from under what she had said.

"Well, how?" he asked again.

Never in her life did she want to say it.

Never in her life could she answer.

She had said too much already.

The answer pounded in her, but it wouldn't come out.

Zeppe-lin-zeppe-lin-

A beam of light grew in her.

The ferns suddenly glowed green. The fronds moved as if shaken by a light puff of wind.

They looked at each other.

He had green shadows on his face.

"Zeppelin," he said softly.

Sitting there, he was the boy in the tree and no one else.

The adults were wrong. She was the one who was right.

The light sank to a green dusk, and the fronds hung windless.

As if nothing had happened.

They looked at each other and smiled.

65

"The adults are talking about a tall thin man with a black cape who steals and does evil things," said Nina. "I don't understand anything. It's so odd when they talk about the shoes in the bedroom and the whistling in the garden. I don't recognize any of it. It's somehow so dangerous when they talk about it. And they don't suspect that it's you."

"Typical," he said seriously.

"And I—I also believed—that you were—the tall thin man."

It was impossible to say more. She couldn't say that she had told Martin about him. That was somehow completely different. Something that didn't have anything to do with them just now.

The boy nodded.

"You weren't in the tree a little while ago," said Nina.

"No, I've been in other places all day, so I haven't heard the news," he answered.

"Well, you can be glad of that. They're all afraid of you. I was frightened, too. Because it really could have been the way the adults were saying—"

He looked at her thoughtfully.

66

"Why did you hide in our house?" asked Nina.

"Perhaps I was escaping from kidnappers," he said.

Nina shook her head.

"Perhaps I'm someone famous in disguise."

Nina didn't believe that either.

"Perhaps I'm hiding from bandits who are after me for information," he said.

That couldn't be true either.

"Perhaps I've run away from cruel foster parents."

Before she started to shake her head, they heard a loud shouting through the fern forest.

67

"Nina! Nina!"

Eva and Martin and other voices.

Nina and the boy quickly glanced at each other.

"They're looking for you," he said softly. "They

mustn't find me now."

"Nina!"

The voices were angry and protective at the same time, loud and strong.

"Hurry back to them before they come over here."

He crept between the ferns on the other side of the stream. She heard his voice: "I don't think they ever do anything but yell at you all the time."

"Nina! Nina!"

Nearer this time.

She felt an urge to follow the boy from the tree. She wanted to disappear into the green fronds. Away from the voices.

She had done something wrong again. She heard it in the voices. Something in the way they called her name. Like the time she had come home after running away. Then the way Eva and Martin had spoken to her had made her feel sad and want to cry.

The ferns were pushed aside. It was Sven.

"So this is where you are?"

It was as if he didn't believe it was true.

"I've found her!" he shouted into the forest.

Sounds grew into a shuffling through the heather and ferns.

Faces peered down at her. Everyone was bewildered. As if they had expected something completely different.

Eva and Martin were there too.

"Nina—"

Martin's voice was happy.

"Nina—"

His voice changed: It was a little angry.

"We've been searching and searching, brought the neighbors with us, because we thought—" Eva interrupted herself.

"Have you been sitting here alone?" Martin was confused now.

Evidently they had expected something else.

"Come," said Martin, "we'd better go home."

Nina stood up. She couldn't look at them.

The others followed. They laughed and talked loudly, as if they were relieved and happy. They must have thought they would find something terrible.

Nina didn't hear what they were talking about. Too much of herself was still there among the ferns. Too many thoughts crept after the boy from the tree.

68

"I don't understand you anymore, Nina. You do exactly the opposite of what we ask."

Nina had to look at Eva. She wasn't angry, but she sat on the sofa and was sad.

Martin wasn't angry either. He looked at Nina as though he wanted to find out if she had become different.

"You frightened us so today," said Eva. "We've

asked you so many times to stay close to the house until we've found out what's going on here."

"You know, it can be dangerous," said Martin. "Perhaps you're too young to understand how dangerous it can be. But we're afraid something might happen to you. We love you, you know. You're our daughter."

"And we are your parents, Nina," said Eva. "I can tell you that something has happened in these past few days that you're keeping secret from us, and I think that's sad. Surely we can help you if anything is wrong."

"Nina, what were you doing in the woods?" asked Martin.

She couldn't answer.

"You know we're afraid that something will happen to you. You must tell us why you went there."

Nina didn't answer.

"Did someone persuade you to go?" he asked.

Nina didn't answer.

"It can be dangerous. We don't even know what's happening in and around our own house," said Eva.

At last she could answer: "It isn't dangerous."

There was total silence.

Friday the fourteenth of July at 4:27 P.M. the bad silence came for a second time.

Eva and Martin stared at her as if they hoped they had not heard what she was saying.

"You don't know anything about it," said Martin, and his voice shook.

Then he lost control. He slammed his fist onto the table, so hard that the noise echoed from the wall.

"And you *will* answer when we ask you something!"

And the questions were thrown at her while the voices became angry and dejected.

69

They were easy questions, but they were impossible.

Nina knew only her own answers.

Eva and Martin wanted to hear theirs.

She had told the truth, but they didn't believe her.

Impossible questions and silence.

70

The rain came in the evening.

Light and blowing.

A strong scent of flowers drifted through the open window.

Eva and Martin watched Nina continually. Wondering looks. Sad looks. Dejected looks. Concerned looks.

They were still waiting for all the answers.

Nina wondered if the boy was sitting in the tree. Probably it was pleasant listening to the patter of the rain on the leaves.

A man stopped at the gate and looked up toward

the house. He didn't open it but remained outside.

He looked around the garden and up toward the house again.

His black umbrella glistened in the rain. Raindrops streamed from its edges.

Then he turned and disappeared down the road.

"What did he want?"

Eva's wondering voice behind Nina. She had not heard Eva coming.

The man wanted something. Nina had noticed that at once.

He had looked into the garden as if he knew what he wanted. As if he were searching for something. As if he didn't dare come and ask.

"Martin," said Eva uneasily. "A man is lurking near our house. He was staring into our garden."

71

Eva came and sat on the edge of Nina's bed.

The rain fell gently on the windowpanes. It was almost dark inside.

"Nina—I just want to say that it isn't easy for us to know what we should believe."

Her face glowed pale in the room.

"We're afraid something will happen to you—"

Her hand stroked the comforter lightly.

"We do what we think is right."

The voice was as soft as the rain outside.

"But perhaps it isn't enough."

Nina had only to stretch out her hand and touch Eva's arm. But she didn't.

Eva stood up. "Good night," she said.

"Good night," answered Nina.

Eva went, and an emptiness grew after her.

72

Moonlight and the July night.
 Gray garden and silver rain.
 Suddenly waking from good dreams.
 Naked feet on the wooden stairs.
 Soft creaking of the wooden floor.
 Hush, at the door—no, no sound.
 And Nina stood under the summer moon
 in the July night and the light of dusk.
 For the first time alone outside on
 a summer night in July dusk
 and moonlight.

73

Alone with the garden she knew during the day.

Alone with the garden that was foreign during the night.

It was like meeting an adventure in reality.

From the window, the garden gave the impression of being gray.

But now—Nina saw glittering rain on the lawn, a

red glow from the roses, shimmering white in the birches, cornflower blue in the shadows and the moon reflected in the windowpanes.

She was alone with the garden.

She didn't think about whether she had permission to be there.

She didn't think about Eva and Martin.

She thought about herself, who had never seen the garden like this.

Perhaps this was how it really was.

Nina's breath quickened. She felt her heart racing.

She and the garden.

She breathed together with the garden.

Her heart beat with the garden's heart.

Thump thump.

Beating through the grass and the sleeping trees.

Beating through the wool bushes and the snow spiraea.

Thump thump.

Zeppe-lin-zeppe-lin-zeppe-lin-

And everything swayed in the garden.

Everything swayed in the word that was beating in the night.

She thought about the boy in the tree.

Then she went out onto the grass and swayed with everything in the garden.

74

"Are you there?"

She whispered between the leaves of silver light.

"Yes, I'm waiting for you. Come up."

Nina had never climbed before, but she gripped the hand he stretched down.

She hauled herself onto the lowest branch, and then it was easy. She climbed up to the boy, who sat between the branches in the green night.

"I knew you would come," he said.

She had to ask him at once—the question that had woken her.

"Was it you who stole Johannes' bicycle?"

"I only borrowed it."

"Did you steal ham and bread from Gerda?"

"I cut two pieces of ham and took two pieces of bread, because I was hungry."

"How did you get in?"

"The same way I got into your house."

"How was that?"

"I can open any lock in the whole world."

Nina looked at him. He wasn't lying.

"Did you also steal the raincoat?"

"It was beginning to rain, and I knew that Svensen had an old raincoat in his boat down by the river. I only borrowed that too. Johannes' bicycle is behind some bushes near the boat."

She believed him. She didn't believe the grown-ups.

"Why do you come to our house?"

He paused at first, but then the answer came.

"Your house is like Sleeping Beauty's castle. Bushes and trees and hedges grow all around, so no one can see whether anyone is living there."

"How long were you in our house?"

"About a week."

"But why are you hiding?"

"I've almost run away from home."

"Almost?"

"Almost."

A little sound from the grass.

They grew still.

The boy carefully moved some branches and peered down.

A dark form glided slowly under them.

The man from the gate.

That was what Nina had felt. He had something to do with the garden and the night and the boy.

He stopped. Almost directly under the tree.

Slowly he lifted his head and looked up.

They carefully let the branches go back into place. They waited. He could not have seen them.

His voice was soft. Almost a whisper. But they heard the words clearly:

"We will try—we can't do anything more than that —now you know—"

They waited a long time, but he didn't say any more.

Carefully they peered between the branches again.

The man was no longer there.

"What did that mean?" whispered Nina.

She was not afraid. Not confused. Not frightened. It was as if such things were supposed to happen in the garden under the tree.

"It was a message," said the boy.

"A message for you?"

He nodded.

75

"There was a special reason why I moved into your house," he said after a while. "The path."

"The path behind the house?" asked Nina.

He nodded.

"It's important for me to be near it."

They sat close to one another. His bare arm touched her arm. A good warmth crept into her.

He was bigger than she was. He was certainly older. Maybe twelve years old. She couldn't ask him about that now.

She stretched out her bare foot so that it touched his shoe.

The *zeppelinshoe*.

All at once she felt a beam of light within her. The same light that was in the July garden and the moonlit night. That was surely why it felt right to sit in a tree in the middle of the night and listen to him talk.

She pulled at a strand of her hair and looked at it.

Spiraea white in the tree.

His hair was black with a silver streak under the moonlit sky.

The branch grew dry where they were sitting. Her pajamas were wet. But it didn't matter.

He continued. His voice was low and close.

"If it becomes serious one day, I will have to use the path."

Nina felt a shiver down her back.

"That path," he said, "that path goes to a secret cave where no one, no one in the whole world, can find me. I'm safe there, and I can live in it until I'm a hundred years old if I must."

"Well, it's not a secret anymore if I know about it," said Nina.

"No one else knows about it," he answered.

"How do I get there?" she asked.

"You can't come there. I'm the only one who knows how to get past all the dangers that lie in wait. First there are four knights with swords made of the sharpest steel that can cut stone and metal. They kill everything that moves on the path— whether it's a mouse or a man."

He watched her as he spoke.

"Then there are four huge wolves that are always hungry. They eat everything that goes by."

She looked at him all the time he spoke.

"Then there's a giant spider with a web across the

path. It's so beautiful that men and animals have to walk right into it when they see it. Then they are trapped there for all eternity."

They watched each other all the time he was speaking.

"Finally there are the tall thin men with black capes who catch children and eat them. And then I arrive at the cave where no one can find me."

He looked down.

"Why are you telling me this?" asked Nina.

He looked up again. His eyes were blue. She couldn't see in the darkness, but she knew it. His eyes had never been dark and dangerous, and they never would be.

"Perhaps because you live near the path, and because it starts in your garden."

A cloud blocked out the moon. For a moment the garden was without light. The great darkness grew out of the forest. Nina huddled close, and a cold draft blew around her ankles.

Then the moon was back.

Their faces were pale.

"I have to go in now," Nina whispered.

His hand stroked her hair and rested on her shoulder.

She let it lie there for a short long second. Then she began to climb down. A big jump to the lawn. The grass felt damp and soft under her feet.

"Meet me in the ferns at noon tomorrow," he whispered to her.

She began to go toward the house.

"And wait." There was a whispering after her. "You might as well bring some food with you when you come."

76

Nina's window looked at her with a moon glance.

Nina looked back.

She stopped on the steps and turned toward the garden.

She listened. Yes, the heartbeat and breathing were still there.

She had wanted to float. She really had floated.

Through the garden. Over the grass. Up in the tree.

One single long feeling of floating.

She stretched out her arms and looked at her fingertips.

I am so big, she thought.

It had never occurred to her before that she had fingertips.

77

Eva and Martin were asleep. Without knowing. Without suspecting anything.

Nina looked at them through a crack in the door.

Far inside her there was something that said she ought to have a bad conscience.

But she didn't.

78

First the voices were far away. Then they came closer. Then she woke up.

Many voices outside the house. Something must have happened, because they were all shouting at the same time.

She stepped out into the yellow rectangular pattern of the sun on the floor and tottered over to the window.

She had slept late today.

She leaned out the window.

Eva and Martin and Sven and Liv were standing on the steps. They were crowded around something. They were talking frantically.

"What is it?" called Nina.

All four looked up.

Sven sneered and mumbled something about the time.

"Look!" said Eva, and dramatically held out her arm.

They drew aside, and Nina saw:

On the steps was a green bicycle with a black raincoat over the handlebars.

"And the worst is," said Martin, "that we have no idea where it came from."

"This is like a nightmare," Eva complained. "Why is it here?"

79

All five stood around the bicycle.

Four were confused.

One was not.

"I don't understand anything," said Martin. "This must be Johannes' bicycle."

"But why is it here?" asked Liv.

"What do they want of us?" said Eva.

"It is almost as if someone were trying to scare you," said Sven.

The bicycle was green with an emblem on its shaft.

Nina said nothing.

80

"You slept so late this morning," said Eva when they were eating breakfast. "Did you sleep well last night?"

"Of course I did," answered Nina.

"I hardly closed my eyes," said Eva.

At any rate they had been closed when Nina had come in from the garden during the night.

81

"Childish pranks," said the policeman when he came to get the bicycle.

"Childish pranks!" Martin snorted angrily. "I don't think these are pranks any longer! This suggests terror to me. And if I get hold of the people who are doing these things, then you can be sure they won't escape!"

"No, it isn't exactly funny anymore," said the policeman, "but what can we do when no one knows anything?"

"This is beginning to be ridiculous," said Martin, and his voice got more and more furious as he spoke. "This is such a small place, and yet there is no one who can do anything about a simple case like this. What will become of us when the law can no longer protect us? What kind of world will we have? Dangerous elements can run around freely and ravage other people's houses and terrorize us so that we can't sleep at night. And now this business of the bicycle!"

Martin took a step toward the policeman.

"Do you know what this means?"

The policeman shook his head.

"I don't either," said Martin, and his voice sank to a whisper. "But I suspect the worst. I'll move heaven and earth to find who's guilty."

Nina looked at him.

Guilty.

Then she was surely one of them.

But she wasn't certain what it was that she had done wrong.

Nina listened.

No heartbeat. No breathing.

No silver or dusk.

Day and night.

Like two different places on the map.

The garden in the daylight was open to everyone. To Eva and Martin and anyone who came and went.

The garden in the nightlight was open to a few. To Nina and the boy in the tree. And to all who swayed in the moonlight.

Eva and Martin slept during the night.

"If we only knew something."

"But we don't know anything."

Nina stared out over the lawn. Past the rose-bushes. Toward the fence and the gate. Farther down the path.

She imagined how the path turned in under the spruce trees. The dark-green light between the ferns. A red flicker of a shirt where someone—

"Nina, what are you smiling about?"

Eva pulled her back from her thoughts.

"You're up to something," said Martin.

"You can't deny it," said Eva.

"Why can't you say what it is?" said Martin.

"I don't like it when you have secrets," said Eva.

Nina closed her eyes. When she only listened to them, they sounded like the children at home in the street. They shrank and were made small by the children's words.

She opened her eyes wide.

"You've spoiled her," said Martin.

"Have I?" said Eva.

"Yes, you're the one who brought her up."

"That's because you didn't want to," said Eva.

"I've never had your permission."

The voices climbed toward anger.

They were both talking at once. Neither of them listened any longer to what the other said.

Nina stood up from the garden table. She felt restless inside. This was the way she believed they spoke to each other behind closed doors. It hurt to listen to them.

She disappeared around the corner of the house to escape from their voices.

84

Nina during the day. Nina during the night.

During the day she was awake. During the night she slept.

One single night she had stayed up.

Not one single day had she slept.

Yesterday was not long ago.

It was not long ago they had sat between the ferns.

It was not long ago that Eva and Martin had searched for her. It was not long ago that they had been angry with her.

Last night was long ago.

It was a long time ago that the garden had been lit in silvery colors. It was a long time ago that she had sat up in the tree and talked with the boy.

When she thought of that time, it was almost like a dream.

85

Really to float.

She had been happy last night.

She stood and wished. That she could sleep during the day and be awake during the night.

Turn everything upside down.

Her heart beat stronger.

Her breathing speeded up.

Dangerous thoughts.

No, no, said Martin in her head.

She ran to the front of the house.

86

Nina stopped short.

Eva and Martin were standing on either side of the garden table.

With unfamiliar faces. With stiff arms.

The end of an argument.

The last words rustled in the grass.

Now they could not pretend that they hadn't argued.

Because now there was no door between them and Nina.

No one had a happy smile, either.

87

Nina couldn't tell them about the green bicycle.

Nina during the night knew about it.

Nina during the day knew nothing.

88

It was five minutes to noon.

The garden was still. The house was still.

Martin had gone off down the road without a word.

Eva had locked herself in the bedroom.

Eva had had enough of Eva.

Martin had had enough of Martin.

No one to call Nina when she went toward the path.

And opened the gate and closed it behind her. And walked under the dark spruce trees.

He was already there.

"Well, what time is this?" he said sternly.

"I—"

"It's five past twelve. If I say twelve, I mean twelve."

Nina looked horrified. He smiled.

"There, there, my friend," he said like a grown-up, "you mustn't get upset when adults tease you."

Nina sat down beside him.

"And where's all the good food you promised to bring along from the royal kitchen?"

The food. She had forgotten the food.

"Oh," he sighed. "I can lie here and die of hunger while you gorge on the world's best dishes and eat yourself to death."

Nina looked at him in amazement.

"It's lucky for me that I can manage without food for months at a time. If I should starve to death, I'd come back from the dead and blame it on you. I would haunt you every single night and drive you mad."

He looked at her and laughed. "You mustn't believe everything I say."

"You— Why did you want me to come here?" asked Nina, who didn't entirely like what they were talking about.

"I haven't finished telling you about being

hungry," he said. "But I can go on with that another time. Come on!"

He got to his feet and made his way between the ferns.

She followed him.

He talked differently during the day.

90

"Hush," he whispered, and lay down on the ground.

Nina did the same.

He crawled through the grass.

Warm earth smells drifted up to them.

He stopped at the top of a knoll. Nina crept up beside him.

A short distance away stood a white house in a field in the middle of the green forest. A little farther away she saw a red house.

"What are we doing here?" she whispered.

He didn't answer.

She looked at the house.

A girl was sitting on the steps working on something. Nina couldn't tell what it was.

A horse pawed the ground by the corner of the house.

A man came out of the stable. Nina thought there was something familiar about him, but she didn't know who he was. He disappeared into the white house.

Suddenly the boy whistled the garden whistle.

The girl on the steps looked up.

He whistled again.

The girl stood up and ran straight toward them as if she knew where they were.

The boy and the girl nodded to one another. She didn't look once at Nina. Nina noticed that she was glad to see the boy.

"Are they still at it?" he asked.

"No, they've finished for the moment," answered the girl.

The boy sighed.

"I meant what I said, you must understand that. Both of them must write it on paper. They *must* promise. Tell them I have to have it in writing."

The girl nodded.

"You can tell them that I'll go even farther away if they don't do it."

"Yes, I'll tell them."

The girl looked at him. Nina suddenly felt sorry for her, because she appeared so helpless.

"I wish you'd come home again soon," the girl said in a low voice.

"I've got money," said the boy, "so I can travel where I want. I broke my piggy bank, and I borrowed money from the chest, but they must have discovered that?"

The girl nodded.

"Were they angry?" he asked.

"No, not exactly. They said they understood."

"Yes, I'm sure they did," the boy said dejectedly, "because they always do. They get two more days, and then that's it. Will you tell them?"

"Yes," answered the girl.

The boy began to snake backward.

"Hurry home, before they guess what you're doing here," he said.

She turned and ran back to the house.

Nina didn't think the girl had noticed her.

The man came out again and looked toward the knoll. But he couldn't see them.

91

The boy didn't say who the girl or the man was.

Nina didn't ask.

He didn't tell her why she was supposed to come along.

Nina didn't ask.

They walked along the path.

He first. She following.

A long silence.

After that some words:

"It was good that you wanted to come with me," he said.

"Will you go up in the tree again?" asked Nina at the gate.

He shook his head.

"I thought you stayed there all the time."

He shook his head.

"But you sleep there?"

"No."

"You said so. Where do you sleep then?"

"Different places—perhaps in a barn."

"But you said—"

"Yes, I say a lot. I always wanted to sleep in the tree, but I never found a way of doing it."

"Why do you sit in the tree at night?"

"Because I'm waiting for you."

She had hoped he would say that.

She was glad he had said it.

"Wait!"

She called after him.

Frightened, she looked up toward the house. No one there.

He turned among the trees.

He came back.

"Why did you leave the bicycle at our house?"

He smiled quickly with his whole face.

"I only wanted to see what the adults would do. A completely ordinary bicycle with a black raincoat on the handlebars. I sat in the tree and watched your mother and father. They shouted and complained as if it were a death machine."

They had also been afraid of the shoes. And the whistling.

"They're just as I thought they would be."

"How?" asked Nina.

"Easily frightened."

He turned and went down the path.

"Why did you think that?" she called after him.

"Because nearly all adults are like that."

"Your parents too?"

"No, they're not afraid of anything."

He was gone.

94

Nina tried again.

"What's your name?" she called softly.

She heard him laughing from inside the forest.

"You don't know what zeppelin means either," he answered.

95

Martin sat on the kitchen steps with nothing in his hands.

That was unusual. Only coffee breaks could get him away from painting and weeding.

It was as if he didn't see Nina right away.

He didn't ask where she had been.

He nodded feebly.

His eyes were kind but sad.

"You've changed since we came here," he said, bewildered. "I can see it in your face. Something has changed in your eyes."

She stood before him.

"I don't understand anything about this summer," he said. "Nothing is as it should be, not even you."

Nina went into the hall.

96

Something distinctive.

Not Ria. Not Otto.

Not Martin. Not Eva.

Something distinctive.

Something Nina.

97

Eva sat at the kitchen table staring into the garden.

She looked tired.

A sad little smile for Nina.

"This summer hasn't been what I hoped," she said. "Everything is different somehow. Not only the summer, but the house and things here as well. I think the rooms change themselves when I go into them. And I'm always afraid something's going to happen. Martin is different—you are too. It frightens me—I wish that this horrible atmosphere would go away so our summer could return."

Eva looked at the garden again.

"Is Martin sitting on the steps?" she asked.

"Yes."

Nothing more.

Nina went outside again.

98

Martin on the steps.

Eva in the kitchen.

He wanted to go inside.

She wanted to go out.

Both stayed where they were.

Nina went into the garden.

99

Tuesday. Wednesday. Thursday. Friday.

Four days.

Only one shower of rain. The rest sunny.

Nina thought back.

She got as far as Monday, the tenth of July, in the evening.

That was the beginning. She was sure of that.

It was then that her bad conscience had begun.

She thought about herself.

Deep inside her there was a small, green, slimy clump of bad conscience.

It had sunk so fast.

It had become small.

Perhaps it would be completely dried out by the

summer sun.

100

Something distinctive.
  Something Nina.

101

"Now he is here again."
  Eva hides behind the curtain.
  Nina leans forward.
  At the gate stands the man from yesterday.
  The man from today. He was the one who had come out of the white house in the forest.
  The man of the moonlight and the silver garden.
  The man with raindrops dripping from the umbrella.
  Without an umbrella he stands at the gate in the setting sun.
  "What does he want?"
  Martin goes out on the front steps.
  The man is not there any longer.
  Only Nina sees that he has gone farther down the road.

102

Eva and Martin were talking together again.
  About the man at the gate.
  What he wanted. Who he was.

Was he the one who—?
The police would be notified tomorrow.
In any case it was a clue.
Something to talk about.
As if nothing had happened earlier that day.

103

Nina woke.
Martin was snoring.
Eva was breathing heavily.
The night was clear with a full moon, and
moonlight reflected on the windowpanes.
Nina and the night were awake.

104

"Hey, you up there—"
"Hey, you down there—"
The foliage closed under her.

105

So odd.
His hands were leaf green between the branches.
Her fingers were white.
She laid her index finger on his hand.
Yes, it was white and green.
His hand over her hair.
A finger glided along the ridge of her nose.
A finger glided over her lips.
She opened her mouth for the tip of her tongue.

His finger tasted of maple and silver moon.

106

"Was that your sister?"

"Yes."

"Was it your father who was here yesterday?"

"Yes."

"I thought you said you'd run away."

"Yes."

"But—no one goes back in the middle of running away."

"Well—I did."

"I don't understand anything."

"No—I don't either—really."

107

"You said it wasn't easy to frighten your parents."

"That's true," he said, a little dejected. "I don't think that they would be afraid even if I ran away."

"Is there any point then?"

"No."

"Why did you run away?"

"Because I thought there was a point."

"Can't you say what then?"

He was quiet for a moment. He lifted his hands to his face and covered his eyes.

"I tried everything. Now there's nothing left to do but run away."

"But why? What have you or they done?"

"I'm trying to get them to understand that they have children."

108

It was surely the night that was to blame.

And the moon. And the silver light. And the stillness around them.

And the tree.

It was surely the night.

The day was for doing things.

The night was for thoughts.

That was how Nina felt.

New thoughts. Other thoughts.

Night thoughts.

109

"They're always calling me," Nina said.

"They never call me," he said.

"They're always asking me what I'm doing and where I am."

"They never ask me what I'm doing or where I am."

"I almost never do what I want."

"I almost always do what I want."

"I never feel really alone."

"I always feel alone."

"They concern themselves with everything I do."

"They never concern themselves with anything I do."

"I wish they didn't always call me," Nina said.

"I wish they called me more often," he said.

"I wish they didn't always ask me where I am and what I'm doing."

"I wish they would sometimes ask me where I am and what I'm doing."

"I wish they would let me do what I wanted."

"I wish they wouldn't always let me do what I wanted."

"I wish they would leave me alone more often."

"I wish they were more concerned about me."

"Do you want to have my parents?" asked Nina.

"No," he answered. "They fret so horribly over you. I want my own parents."

"But you ran away from them."

"I like them all the same."

"Well, I like my mother and father, but I wish they liked me the way I am. Perhaps I should run away too."

He looked at her thoughtfully.

"You have already run away," he said.

She looked back at him.

Then she nodded.

"I certainly have," she said.

"Don't they understand that they have children?" asked Nina.

He shook his head.

"No, they think too much about themselves. There's always something wrong. They're always arguing. Mother is always packing a bag and disappearing. Father is always going after her and bringing her home again. Always. Always."

"Then I understand why you ran away," said Nina.

"I've asked them to stop fighting. Yes, they answer, but then they forget it again right afterward. Once I said that I would jump out of the window if they didn't stop. That was in the middle of the night, and I couldn't sleep because of their quarreling."

"Did you do it?"

"Yes, I did. I even broke my leg, but they still went on exactly the same afterward."

"Have you tried anything else?"

"I said I would smash their best set of dishes if there weren't some quiet in the house."

"Did you do it?"

"Yes, but I didn't smash all the dishes. They stopped me before I could finish. But during the night they went on arguing. So I got up and smashed the rest."

"Were they angry?"

"Yes—and that is what's so unfair."

"What was it your father said in the garden yesterday?"

"He said that they would try to stop the arguing and all the nonsense."

"Are you going home?"

"No, not before they promise to stop arguing and making trouble, and they have to promise that they'll think more about my sister and me and not only about themselves. And they have to promise to be nice to each other. I want to have that in writing, so I can show it to them if they forget."

"What's going to happen the day after tomorrow?"

"If they don't promise in black and white, I'm shoving off for good."

"Where to?"

"I'm not telling."

113

Nina knew where.

The cave in the forest.

The cave that lay beyond all the dangers.

Then Nina knew that it was serious.

114

The vacation house was glowing white in the summer night.

Martin was snoring.

The summer night glowed with a blue light in the

vacation house.
Eva was breathing heavily.
Nina floated.
White in the summer night.
Blue in the vacation house.
Floating and sleeping toward daybreak.

115

Zeppelin was a sun.
Zeppelinfreckles over the whole body.
They came out in all summer's colors.
And she rocked. Back and forth.
Zeppelinsong.
Nina—Nina—Nina—
Then she woke up.
Eva was there and carefully shaking her.
"Are you catching something?" she asked her.
Nina didn't exactly grasp what she said.
The sun was still glowing too strongly in her.

116

"The bicycle!" roared Martin.
"The bicycle!"
Eva and Nina came to the window.
"This cannot be true!" screamed Eva.
Against the steps stood a green bicycle with an emblem on the shaft.
"But Johannes' bicycle was returned to him yesterday. What does this mean? I demand that this

be cleared up!"

"Martin," said Eva, "this can't be true."

"But here it is, real as day," said Martin, "just listen."

And he rang the bicycle bell.

117

The policeman came. The policeman went.

He didn't understand a thing.

Johannes didn't know anything.

The bicycle had been outside his house the evening before.

No one knew what it meant.

Only Nina.

She had seen how they became angry and afraid.

Even though it was only a green bicycle.

118

One day left.

Tomorrow would be serious business.

Suddenly Nina knew what she had to do.

The *zeppelindream* had given her the answer.

She understood why he had taken her home with him yesterday.

She had to try to rescue him from the cave.

If he went there, it would be too late to save him.

119

The neighbors came in droves.

They hung over the fence or sat on the grass or on

the veranda.

They were all puzzled about what had happened.

Childish pranks, they said bravely, but there was an ever-so-slight tone of uncertainty in their voices.

No one noticed that Nina had disappeared through the gate at the back of the house.

120

She wanted to walk straight to the white house in the forest.

She wanted to go straight up the steps and knock on the door.

She wanted to say straight out that they had to do as the boy asked.

But she didn't dare.

Nina slowed down when the white house appeared between the trees.

She sat down on the knoll. There she was partly concealed and partly visible.

The man came out of the house. He stopped on the steps and looked at the knoll. He caught sight of her. Slowly he walked over to the knoll.

Now she couldn't run away.

121

"Well, well, so you came alone?" he said, looking around in surprise.

"Yes," answered Nina. "He doesn't know that I'm here."

"Oh, no—"

Nina didn't know what she should say. All the brave words she had thought up on the path were suddenly gone.

"Isn't he coming home?" the man asked carefully.

Nina shook her head.

"He's not coming?"

The man was sad.

"He will come only if you promise in writing what he has asked you."

He looked at her.

"You know a lot, don't you?" he said.

"He told me everything," answered Nina.

"That's not quite true," said the man, "because he doesn't know everything."

122

"How did you know he was in our garden?" asked Nina.

The man smiled a little.

"I guessed when I heard the strange rumors."

"But how did you know that he was sitting in the tree?"

The man glanced passed her. Toward the forest. Toward the path.

"Summer nights," he said. "He takes after me."

Nina waited for him to say more.

"I too have wandered under the moon on summer nights."

His voice was distant, as if it came from long ago.

"He wasn't wandering," said Nina. "He was sitting in a tree."

Again the man smiled gently at her.

"The maple is the thickest tree in your garden. It has the finest branches, and therefore has the best lookout in all directions. That's why I thought he would be there. And there's one more thing."

Nina waited.

"It's a good tree to be in."

Nina gave him a slight nod.

She agreed about that.

It grew quiet between them.

123

They sat on the garden bench under the tall birch.

Sounds came from the open window.

Was it the mother who was there?

Were the sounds angry?

Had they argued and become enemies again?

He appeared to be gentle and peaceful.

As if he couldn't argue with anyone in the whole world.

124

"Hello, we have a visitor."

Brown arms and a smiling face at the window.

A smile that was also in her eyes.

She looked at Nina with kindness.

"I know who you are," she said. "You have lent your tree to our son."

125

All three sat on the garden bench under the birch.

His parents.

They were not as she had thought his parents would be.

Nina couldn't imagine that the mother would just run away.

She couldn't imagine that they would be enemies.

They sat close to each other.

Right up against each other.

Nina thought about Eva and Martin.

Martin on the steps.

Eva in the kitchen.

Far from each other.

126

"I don't even know his name," said Nina.

"Didn't he tell you?"

The woman smiled a little.

"I can imagine that," said the man. "I'm sure he'll tell you when he wants you to know."

127

"My name is Eli."

"My name is Oscar."

"My name is Nina."

128

"You must persuade him to come home again. Tell him everything will be fine."

"That's not enough," said Nina. "He wants you to promise that you will never again—"

Suddenly she couldn't say it.

She blushed and looked down.

129

"We know what he wants us to promise," said Eli.

"He feels that we forget that we have children," said Oscar, "and that we think too much about ourselves."

"Yes, and tomorrow it will be serious if you don't do as he says," said Nina.

"Serious?" Oscar looked at her with alarm.

"What does that mean?" Eli was anxious.

"I can't say," Nina answered firmly.

130

"We love our son and daughter," said Oscar.

"We happen to argue, and occasionally we part, but it isn't always so serious," said Eli.

"No, not always," said Oscar, and looked at Eli.

"It's not only my fault," she said, and a wrinkle appeared on her forehead.

"No, well, I didn't say that either."

"But you meant it—"

"No, I didn't."

"Let's not pursue this now," Eli said more calmly. "We have a visitor, after all."

A bit confused, they looked at Nina.

"As you can see," said Oscar, "we easily get steamed up, and we both want to be in the right."

"Yes, especially one of us," said Eli.

Oscar fell silent.

"Perhaps we shouldn't have gotten married after all?" said Eli, looking at Oscar.

He returned her look. "But we are married," he said. "And we are fond of each other in spite of everything, aren't we?"

Eli smiled at him. She smiled a little more at Nina.

"There, you see," she said. "It's difficult to make an effort even for one's own sake."

They spoke as if she understood.

"He says you only think of yourselves," said Nina.

They were silent.

131

"Poor boy," said Eli, "just think that we are forcing him to run away from home. It isn't easy to be young and anxious."

"He isn't young and anxious," said Nina. "He's big and brave and dares to do many things."

They looked at her.

"We evidently know him in different ways," said Oscar quietly.

"Shall we tell you what we think?" asked Eli.

"Yes," answered Nina.

"He wants everything safe and calm around him. Everyone should be nice to each other. Even when we are only discussing something, he thinks we are enemies."

"If he had his way," said Oscar, "he would lock himself in a place where he could huddle and not hear the least sound."

"He's nice to his sister even though she's only nine, three years younger than he is. Sometimes they even play her games," said Eli.

"He's very young for his age even if he is beginning to grow up."

Nina had not known that.

132

"But our son is also brave," said Oscar. "I understand very well why he ran away."

"Aren't you angry about that?" asked Nina in surprise. She remembered the time she had run away.

"No," said Eli, "but I feel that he should come home now."

Nina looked puzzled.

Oscar smiled at her.

"It's becoming difficult," he said.

Nina didn't answer.

"The wonderful thing about our son is that he always does what he says."

Nina thought about the time he had jumped out of the window and when he had smashed the dinner set.

"Last week something happened again that made us say more to each other than we meant. It was then he said that he couldn't bear it anymore. He wanted to take off. And he did."

"He'll come back only if you think more about him," said Nina. "He can't stand the bickering and noise and arguing. It makes him sad and it hurts him and he'll scream and cry and kick and hit and behave as if it isn't true and—"

Nina stopped, suddenly quiet.

He hadn't said any of this.

It was the way she felt whenever she thought Eva and Martin were arguing.

It was herself she was talking about.

133

"We can't promise that," said Oscar.

"We can only do our best," said Eli.

"He has to accept that we love him and care about him. I don't understand when he says that we don't realize we have children. Because we surely know that."

Nina heard that they were making things seem

simpler than they were.

He wouldn't come back again.

"That's not enough," she said. "Tomorrow it will be serious."

They looked at her, bewildered.

Now it was getting difficult for them.

134

Nina turned around.

The knoll hid the house.

She took some steps back.

The house was still there.

So she really had been there.

135

"Tonight," said Martin.

"Tonight," said Eva.

"Tonight I will stay awake. If the police can't do anything, then I'll have a try. And I won't be gentle when I get hold of whoever is messing us about."

Tonight, thought Nina.

136

White-outlined black clouds.

Threat of rainy weather over the garden.

Nina woke.

Barefoot over the floor.

Eva was sleeping alone.

Carefully down the stairs.

Martin was sleeping and keeping watch at the kitchen table.

Out into the garden shifting in black and silver.

A rustling crept through the grass and between the leaves.

A wind that preceded rain.

137

The branches swung heavily.

"I've been at your parents' house," said Nina. "They can't promise anything."

He turned his face toward the tree trunk.

The leaves rustled around them.

"Then there's only one thing to do," he whispered. "They asked for it."

One thing to do—

Desperation grew inside her.

She could not stop him going to the cave.

138

"Your parents were nice," she said softly. "They talked to me as if I were not me."

Yes, that's how it was.

"I wish my mother and father could be more like them."

"I'm never going home again," he said. "I just can't

do it."

"They care about you," said Nina.

"Then why don't they show it! I'm always afraid that they'll get angry with each other again. I wake up during the night and I'm afraid—and it doesn't matter what I say. They don't listen to me. As if I weren't there. They only push me aside as if I'm in the way. The next day they say that they love me. But I want them to like me all the time. Not only when they want to! And it can't just be something they say. They have to mean it, too!"

Was he crying?

Nina wasn't sure.

"I can't bear it that they're angry with each other and argue and forget that we're also—"

He didn't get any further.

Through the sighing of the wind and the moonlight came a desperate scream.

Naked and white.

"Martin! Nina has disappeared!"

The two in the tree looked at each other.

Their eyes were big and afraid.

The door was thrown open.

Two forms ran out into the night.

Out into Nina's night.

139

"Nina!"

The voice floated in the wind and became distant.

Eva and Martin.

Nightgown and pajamas.

Whirring around.

Helplessly in circles.

"Nina!"

The two peered down from the tree.

Back and forth over the grass.

Between the bushes and the trees.

"Nina!"

Eva was crying. Nina heard it.

"What has happened, Martin?"

"How do I know?"

Heated and angry. Afraid and anxious.

The wind tugged at their clothes.

"Has the man taken her?"

"I told you I haven't the faintest idea."

Back and forth again.

They were searching without searching.

They didn't float through the garden.

They tramped around with a daytime stride.

"But you must have heard her get up!" screamed Martin over by the peonies.

"And you were supposed to be keeping watch!" Eva shouted back from the lilac bushes.

"You were nearest to her!"

"You were nearest to the back door!"

The words were chopped up by the wind. Spun around the entire garden. Down in the grass. Into the bushes. Up in the trees. Up to those two.

Nina sat stiffly and listened. Didn't dare look at the boy.

Now and then she looked at her parents.

Eva and Martin. But they were not Eva and Martin.

She sat in the tree and looked at two people she didn't recognize.

They seemed small and insignificant.

"Where can she be—?"

"What has happened—?"

"... the police, Martin—"

"... the most frightful thing—"

"... our daughter—"

Words torn loose blew up to them.

The voices were desperate.

Nina could simply jump down to them and say: "Here I am."

She could make them happy again.

But she stayed where she was.

She hung on to the swaying branch.

She didn't know what she should do.

Back and forth they ran.

Like birds with ruined wings—

Like leaves without direction—

They whirled around without thinking.

Without knowing what to do.

"No one can have come into the house or we would have heard them." Martin tried to console himself and Eva.

"But then—then she must have gone of her own accord," said Eva. "But why?"

"It's your fault," shouted Martin. "You're the one who's brought her to what she is!"

Silence.

"Are you listening to what I'm saying?"

Martin's voice rose with the wind.

He was a wind troll. A garden scarecrow. A night spirit. He was no longer Martin.

"If there is anyone to blame," said Eva firmly and calmly, but the tone of voice reached the two up in the tree, "then it is both of us and not just me."

"But, but it was you—"

"No," shrieked Eva, interrupting him, "it is our child, don't you understand that?"

Like looking at TV.

Like reading a book.

But different just the same.

Nina saw something that was a part of her.

"Nina! Please! Where are you?"

As if they were playing hide and seek.

Home-free-all and everything would be fine.

You won't move because no one is smiling anymore.

Eva stopped and lifted her face toward the moon and the heavens.

"Nina, please—"

But Nina stayed still.

She was not paralyzed. But the tree was a world apart from these people who were shouting and running around in the garden.

Martin stopped a short distance away.

"There's no point in shrieking like that. You'll only wake the neighbors."

Then Eva started crying loudly.

Long, loud sobbing that shook her body.

"You don't understand anything," she sobbed.

Martin went to her.

His arms were open.

"Don't touch me!" shrieked Eva.

Martin froze in the summer's night wind.

Eva didn't move.

As if time had stopped.

Nina and the boy looked at each other.

His face was striped with tears.

Then Nina climbed down.

It was the only thing she could do.

140

"Nina!"

Martin spoke in a dream.

Eva looked at her in a dream.

"Nina!"

Eva tried to stretch out her arms, but they wouldn't obey.

"Where have you been?"

"What happened?"

Martin came slowly to himself again.

"You'd better answer, child!"

He came toward her.

Eva came after him.

Nina pressed herself against the tree trunk.

"Nina," said Eva in a low voice, "I don't under-stand—"

"Did you creep out simply to frighten us?"

Martin's voice rose.

Their eyes met.

Garden scarecrow. Wind troll.

The garden at night was not for Eva and Martin.

Nina spread out her arms as if she were protecting the tree behind her.

It was as if Martin suddenly understood some-thing.

"What were you doing in that tree?"

"The tree?" said Eva. "Have you been there all the time we were screaming and shrieking? Nina, what is happening to you?"

Both of them came toward her.

They grew and grew. Their hands became glowing white claws.

They came from the day.

And Nina had believed she could help them by coming down from the tree.

They stamped toward her.

She heard the silvery garden being smashed under their feet.

"No-o-o-o!" she shouted.

"What were you doing in the tree?"

Martin's arms shook her.

"Answer me! You *shall* answer me! You've been quiet a whole week, but now I shall have an answer!"

"Martin!" shouted Eva. "What are you doing?"

Abruptly, he let her go.

"I shall find out for myself," he said, and went over to the tree.

"No," shouted Nina.

She threw herself at Martin and tried to hold him.

Martin was taken by surprise. He stopped and looked at her.

"What does this mean?" Eva barely whispered.

"You aren't allowed! You aren't allowed!"

Nina was screaming just as loudly as they had done.

"I shall!" Martin broke loose, but Nina came at him again.

She held on and clawed and kicked.

"Nina, what is the matter with you!"

He tried to shake himself free again, but she didn't give up.

"You aren't allowed! You aren't allowed!"

She shrieked until her throat was sore. The words shot out over the garden, over the hedges.

Over to the neighbors.

Lights were turned on in houses. Doors were

opened.

Suddenly a shadow jumped down from the other side of the tree.

"Look there!" shouted Eva, and pointed.

The form shot over the lawn toward the back of the house.

Martin wanted to go after it, but Nina held him.

She cried and called out: "No, no!"

Because Martin wanted to go up into the tree.

Because he wanted to go after the boy from the tree.

Because she heard the gate to the path slamming in the wind.

Because she would never see the boy again.

Voices reached her. Feet through the grass. Flashlights.

The neighbors had come.

"What is it?"

"What's going on?"

Again they were all talking at once.

Nina just lay on the lawn.

She noticed the lights from some of the flashlights disappearing in the direction of the gate.

141

The rest of the night was voices and questions and coffee cups.

Nina lay under the comforter and heard the voices below.

Eva came up and sat on the edge of the bed.

She tried to talk, but Nina said not a word.

Then a doctor arrived and examined her.

And suddenly it was morning with sun and warmth.

142

They tried everything.

With kindness, with desperation. They even used a few threats.

Nina was silent.

She didn't see them.

She sat straight up in a chair and was not present.

Then the police came.

And the neighbors.

And others.

They wanted to search the whole neighborhood and the forest nearby.

They set out.

Eva and Nina were left alone.

Nina knew they wouldn't find him.

Martin came home worn out after many hours of searching.

He looked at Nina as if she were a stranger.

Nina continued to sit silently in the chair.

143

Later in the afternoon the policeman came back.

The three adults sat down beside Nina.

The policeman cleared his throat and spoke.

"Do you want to tell us what happened?"

Nina stared out of the window.

"Did he lure you out of the house?"

There was no wind in the trees now.

"Did he do something to you?"

"What did he talk about?"

"You understand it is important that we find him," said the policeman. "What he has done is very serious."

"What has he done?" asked Nina.

They were surprised that she had suddenly spoken.

"He—" The policeman hesitated.

"You don't understand anything!" said Nina.

"Nina, please!"

Martin and Eva were aghast.

But Nina was silent again.

144

In the late-evening dusk there was a knock at the door.

It was the man who had stood at the gate.

Eva looked uncertainly at him.

He caught sight of Nina and smiled.

"Hi," he said.

"Hi," answered Nina.

Alarmed, Eva looked at her. And then at the man.

"I believe I must clear up some misunderstandings," said the man.

"Oh?" said Martin, puzzled.

"Yes. I've heard the latest rumors, and now it has become so serious that I must do something about it. I also need help from your daughter."

"From Nina!"

Eva looked mistrustfully at him.

"Yes. She's the only one who knows where I can find my son."

145

After that they looked in astonishment at Nina.

"Why didn't you tell us this?"

"You've frightened us terribly."

Nina continued to say nothing.

The man looked at her. She looked back.

"Perhaps she wasn't allowed to tell," he said.

"Not allowed!"

"But, Nina, how can you believe—"

But she didn't answer.

146

"What shall we do now?"

It was Eva who asked.

"We have to try to get my son back again," answered Oscar.

"Yes, I think so too," Martin said. "I think he deserves a spanking after what he's done."

"Well, he has certainly given you a scare," said

Oscar. "Do you know where he is, Nina?"

She nodded.

"Will you go and get him?"

She shook her head.

"But Nina, you have to," said Eva crossly.

"He has to decide for himself whether he wants to come," said Nina.

Oscar nodded. "But you can go to him and say that we want him to come back."

"I'm not going if he'll be punished, because he hasn't done anything wrong."

"Not done anything—"

Martin couldn't believe his ears.

"No, he hasn't done anything. You must believe that. If you promise that you won't punish him, perhaps I can go."

Martin was silent.

"Do you promise?"

He looked at her with an amazed stare.

Oscar and Eva waited for an answer.

"Do you promise?" she asked again.

"Can't you do that, Martin? After all, he's only a young boy," said Eva.

"I don't think he should get away with this," said Martin.

"In that case I'm not going," Nina said firmly.

"Martin—" pleaded Eva.

"It's really not so dangerous," said Oscar.

"Are you all against me?" said Martin, bewildered.

No one said anything.

They all waited.

"All right, all right," said Martin. "I'll have to give in, but I must be allowed to tell him that he must not do this anymore. Is that okay?"

"If you say it without getting angry," answered Nina.

"All right, I'll try," said Martin, but grudgingly.

Oscar looked at her. "Can you ask him to come home to us? We can only do our best. Say to him that in any case we can try to talk about things. I can't promise that everything will be fine from now on."

Nina nodded.

147

"Do you dare to go there?"

It was Martin who asked.

Nina thought about the path.

She thought about the knights. About the wolves. About the giant spider. About the tall thin men in black capes.

Did she dare?

She was the only person who could go. The only one who knew the way.

She understood why he had told her about the path and the cave and the dangers.

He wanted her to bring him back if it became serious one day.

He was depending on her.

She must trust him.

He wouldn't have told her if he didn't believe that she could overcome the dangers.

"Perhaps it would be best if I came with you," said Martin.

She had to go alone.

"Perhaps I can follow you a little way—"

There was a hint of something in his voice she hadn't heard before.

Nina nodded. That would be fine, just in case.

She stood up and looked for a flashlight in the closet.

Martin followed her to the door.

"Nina—"

She turned around.

Eva looked at her with eyes shining through tears. Then she shook her head and looked down at the table. She didn't say any more.

148

They went around the house toward the gate.

Between the trees it was dark.

The great darkness she was afraid of.

Martin walked behind her on the path.

He didn't know what he should say.

He couldn't stroke her hair as he really wanted.

He couldn't pat her shoulder.

He felt strange walking behind Nina.

Usually it was the other way around.

They came to where the path stopped.

Nina switched on the flashlight and pointed it at the heather.

The path didn't stop after all. A small trail led into the heather. That was where she should go.

"You can wait here," said Nina.

"Do you dare to go alone then?" he asked.

"Yes," she answered.

"You just shout if you get frightened or there is anything."

"Yes," she answered.

"I'll wait here then," he said.

Nina set off.

He saw the beam of light from the flashlight bobbing ahead of her.

Some new thoughts had come into his head.

He didn't want to think them.

He didn't know how he could think them.

Thoughts about being big and little.

Nina was big as she went into the darkness of the forest.

"Father?" she called.

"Yes," he answered.

"Do you dare to stand there alone?"

"Yes," he answered confidently. Then he added softly: "I think so."

The forest grew thicker.

The path became clear again.

The darkness sifted down between the branches.

She was afraid.

Her heart and her breath were afraid.

But in the back of her heartbeat was the sound:

Zeppe·lin·zeppe·lin·

So she went on.

A weak beam of light from the flashlight.

The moon did not reach down between the trees.

Hush—what was that?

There was a soft clattering.

Someone drew a sword.

The four knights.

She went on. She didn't look to the side.

Two black bushes on either side of the path.

She could not pass.

She had to pass.

At once, she knew how.

"*Zeppelin,*" she said.

The swords fell clattering to the ground, and the bushes grew lighter.

The path turned down a slope.

It went around a big stone that blocked the way.

Rustling in the heather. Something moved in the bushes. Something scraped against the tree stumps.

A threatening, low growl. And suddenly the light

reflected sharp white teeth.

Zeppelin, she thought.

The growling stopped, and the bushes grew still.

Onward.

The little beam of light moved before her on the path.

Then the trees opened on a small green clearing.

The moon sent down light that glittered in threads. A little melody came faintly to her.

It was beautiful.

She knew what was coming, but she could not turn back.

The music grew stronger. The threads shone yellow. She could not get away.

Zeppelin, she thought.

A cloud drifted in front of the moon. The colors faded, and the music became the sighing of the wind. Something tickled her leg. She walked through a spider's web.

Into the thick forest again.

Very soon she heard a rustling and crackling along the path.

She noticed shadows stretching out to become long and thin.

They joined together along the path and grew in the big dangerous darkness. The darkness was their capes.

Zeppelin, she thought.

Rustling, the darkness glided into dusk.

Then she arrived.

A mountain knoll in the middle of the forest.

A black silhouette against the sky.

The path led to the opening of a cave.

"It's me," she said.

"Yes," he answered.

"They want you to come home."

He didn't answer.

"You won't get a beating or punishment or anything," she said, "I made them promise that."

He didn't answer.

"Your father and mother miss you. They can only do their best, they say."

He didn't answer.

"They want you to come home all the same."

He didn't answer.

She thought about the hundred years he would be in the cave.

"I will be here the whole summer," Nina said carefully, "and I thought that maybe we could be friends—"

She waited, but he didn't answer.

"Are you coming home now?"

"Perhaps—"

"We can't use the tree any longer. They've discovered it, but we can find another place."

"I know one," he said.

"Are you coming now?" she asked again.

"No," he answered, "I don't know."

She began to go back along the path.

"Are you leaving?" he said.

"Yes. My father's waiting for me," she said.

The boy was quiet. She stood still.

"You don't even know my name," he said.

"No, but I know who you are," she replied.

She walked away through the trees.

His voice reached her:

"You don't know what zeppelin means either!"

"No," she called back, "but I know how it works."

Then there was silence.

Back along the path.

Suddenly the moon reached down between the trees.

And Nina switched the flashlight off.